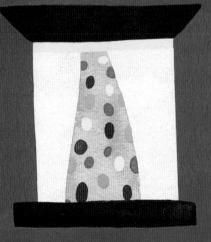

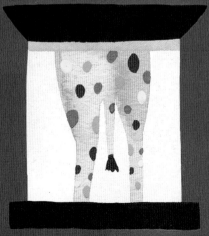

To Daisy

THIS IS A BORZOI BOOK PUBLISHED BY ALFRED A. KNOPF

Copyright © 2020 by Sarah Williamson

All rights reserved. Published in the United States by Alfred A. Knopf, an imprint of Random House Children's Books, a division of Penguin Random House LLC, New York.

Knopf, Borzoi Books, and the colophon are registered trademarks of Penguin Random House LLC.

Visit us on the Web! rhcbooks.com

Educators and librarians, for a variety of teaching tools, visit us at RHTeachersLibrarians.com

Library of Congress Cataloging-in-Publication Data is available upon request.
ISBN 978-0-525-64881-9 (trade) — ISBN 978-0-525-64882-6 (lib. bdg.) — ISBN 978-0-525-64883-3 (ebook)

The illustrations in this book were created using gouache paint and pastels.
Book design by Elizabeth Tardiff

MANUFACTURED IN CHINA
November 2020
10 9 8 7 6 5 4 3 2 1
First Edition

ELEVATOR BIRD

Sarah Williamson

Alfred A. Knopf 🐾 New York

THE HOTEL

*all are welcome!
*stay for a day... or more!

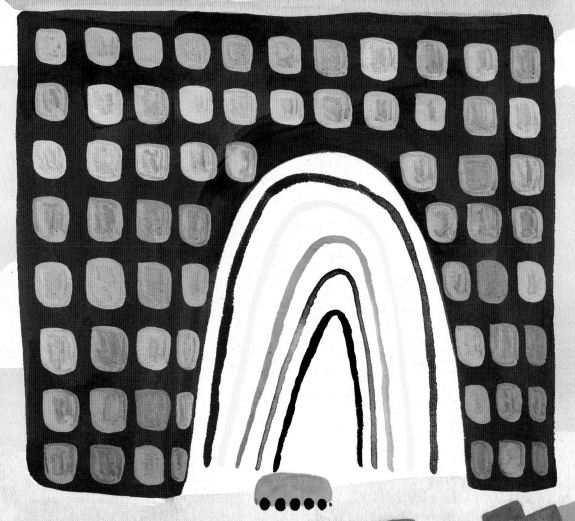

This is Elevator Bird.
He works at the hotel.

Hello!

It takes a big team to run the hotel.

Mr. Rumpley is the hotel manager.
He makes sure everything goes smoothly.

The worms are the porters.
They handle everyone's luggage with great care.
They love to say, "Let us help you with that!"

Raffi does the maintenance.
Everyone likes him because
he can fix anything!

Randy is the chef.
He bakes the croissants, custard tarts,
cranberry muffins, and cupcakes. He also
makes an excellent eggplant Parmesan.

Ally is the host at the hotel
restaurant, Randy's Place. She greets
and seats all of the guests.

Jane and Olivia are the receptionists.
They check in each guest and ask everyone,
"How may we help you?" and say, "It's our pleasure."

Mousey does housekeeping.
He makes the hotel sparkle by getting into
every nook and cranny.

THE HOTEL
*starters
red hot chili
peppers
nachos with
queso
*mains
Randy's eggplant
parmesan
Grilled cheese

Esther is the server at Randy's Place.
She waits on the guests hand and foot.

Charlie washes the dishes.
"It's a dirty job, but someone's got to do it,"
he says with a smile.

It's Elevator Bird's job to take the guests up and down and to welcome everyone, tall and small.

Welcome to the elevator!

He is very polite.

Hold the door, please.

Sure thing, wormies!

Elevator Bird always has a kind word for everyone. And he certainly is very helpful.

When the work is done, Elevator Bird goes to the basement. His quarters are cramped and creaky, but his good pal Mousey keeps him company. Yet something is missing. . . .

Still, each day Elevator Bird sends
the guests off with good cheer.

Have fun at Boo Gardens!

He knows the city like the back of his wing,
and he makes lots of helpful recommendations.

You must
go to Sonny Skye's
Rooftop Restaurant!

Turn right on Fox Lane,
left on Cherry Road, and
you'll be at Peacock Place.
The views are magnificent.

Each night, Elevator Bird goes back to the basement. He loves his job, but he wishes he could get out more. Elevator Bird longs for dark nights filled with city lights.

A room with a view sure would be nice, Mousey!

Oh, yes?

Mousey tells Mr. Rumpley
Elevator Bird's wish.

Mr. Rumpley calls everyone together for a secret meeting, and they hatch a plan.

Shh... don't tell! It's a surprise!

plants

wood

paint

pencil

bucket

nails

hammer

poles

ladder

lights

candy

jar

ladle

Operation Elevator Bird

roll of paper

hot-air
balloon

sunglasses

cones

broom

pitcher

paintbrush

hat

cups

stool

peanut butter
and jelly
sandwiches

disguise

work boots

bowl

crane

The worms are on crane duty.

Raffi goes out for supplies.

PAINT store

Randy gets the candy.
Randy eats the candy.
Randy, don't eat the candy!

Charlie strings the lights.

That day, everyone takes the stairs.

The day is very quiet, but Elevator Bird
keeps busy with his feather duster.

Everyone piles in.

Oh my! What a sight to see.

Sweet delight! Mr. Rumpley and the gang
have made a new home for Elevator Bird right
up on the roof! He hardly knows what to say.

It's all for you, Elevator Bird!

Enjoy!

Quelle surprise!
I can hardly believe it.
Look at this view—I love it!

Congratulations, Elevator Bird

Elevator Bird

Now Elevator Bird has the view he's always dreamed of because of his best friends. And, in the glow of the starlight, he wishes everyone at the hotel a good night.